GEORGE AND MARTHA
THE BEST OF FRIENDS

For My Mother

The stories in this book were originally published
by Houghton Mifflin Company in
George and Martha: Round and Round.
Copyright © 1988 by James Marshall
Copyright © renewed 2000 by Sheldon Fogelman

www.houghtonmifflinbooks.com

Library of Congress Cataloging-in-Publication Data

Marshall, James, 1942–1992.
George and Martha : the best of friends /
written and illustrated by James Marshall.
p. cm.
"The stories in this book were originally published by Houghton Mifflin
Company in George and Martha round and round"–T.p. verso.
Summary: Two stories chronicle the ups and downs of a special friendship
between two hippopotamuses.
ISBN-13: 978-0-618-98451-0
[1. Friendship–Fiction. 2. Hippopotamus–Fiction.] I. Title.
PZ7.M35672Gce 2008
[E]–dc22
2007025741

TWP 10 9 8 7 6 5 4 3 2 1
Printed in Singapore

GEORGE AND MARTHA
THE BEST OF FRIENDS

written and illustrated by
JAMES MARSHALL

HOUGHTON MIFFLIN COMPANY BOSTON

TWO STORIES ABOUT THE BEST OF FRIENDS

STORY NUMBER ONE

THE ATTIC

One cold and stormy night
George decided to peek into the attic.
"Go on up," said Martha.
"Oooh no," said George.
"There might be a ghost up there,
or a skeleton, or a vampire,
or maybe even some werewolves."
"Oooh goody!" said Martha.
"Let's investigate."

But there wasn't much to see in the attic—
only a box of old rubber bands.

George was disappointed.

"Would you like to hear a story that will
give you goose bumps?" asked Martha.

"You bet," said George.

"When you hear it, your bones will go cold,"
said Martha.

"Oooh," said George.

"Your blood will curdle," said Martha.

"Ooooh," said George.

"And you'll feel mummy fingers up and
down your spine," said Martha.

"Stop!" cried George. "I can't take any more.
Tell me some other time!"

That night Martha went to bed
with the light on.
She had a bad case of goose bumps.

STORY NUMBER TWO

THE SURPRISE

One late-summer morning
George had a wicked idea.
"I shouldn't," he said.
"I really shouldn't."
But he just couldn't help himself.
"Here comes the rain!" he cried.
"Egads!" screamed Martha.

Martha was thoroughly drenched
and as mad as a wet hen.

"That did it!" she said.

"We are no longer on speaking terms!"

"I was only horsing around,"
said George.

But Martha was unmoved.

The next morning, Martha read a funny story.
"I can't wait to tell George," she said.
Then she remembered that she and George
were no longer on speaking terms.
Around noon Martha heard a joke
on the radio.
"George will love this one," she said.
But she and George weren't speaking.
In the afternoon Martha observed
the first autumn leaf fall to the ground.
"Autumn is George's favorite season," she said.
Another leaf came swirling down.
"That does it," said Martha.

Martha went straight to George's house.

"I forgive you," she said.

George was delighted to be back
on speaking terms.

"Good friends just can't stay cross for
long," said George.

"You can say that again," said Martha.
And together they watched the
autumn arrive.

But when summer rolled around again,
Martha was ready and waiting.

JAMES MARSHALL (1942–1992)
is one of the most popular and celebrated
artists in the field of children's literature.
Three of his books were selected as New
York Times Best Illustrated Books, and he
received a Caldecott Honor Award in 1989
for *Goldilocks and the Three Bears*. With more
than seventy-five books to his credit, includ-
ing the popular George and Martha series,
Marshall has earned the admiration and
love of countless readers.